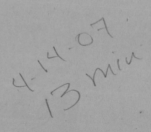

4-14-07
13 min

What Will Mommy Do When I'm at School?

written and illustrated by Dolores Johnson

Atheneum Books for Young Readers

To Robbie, Alix, Alan, and Kaci

Atheneum Books for Young Readers   An imprint of Simon & Schuster Children's Publishing Division, 1230 Avenue
of the Americas, New York, New York 10020   Copyright © 1990 by Dolores Johnson   All rights reserved including
the right of reproduction in whole or in part in any form.

Printed and bound in Hong Kong   First American Edition   10 9 8 7 6 5 4

The text of this book is set in 18 point Garamond No. 3.
The illustrations are rendered in watercolor and colored pencil on paper.

Library of Congress Cataloging in Publication Data   Johnson, Dolores. What will Mommy do when I'm in school?
Summary: A child worries about how her mother will cope at home on her own while she is at school. [1. Mothers –
Fiction] I. Title.   PZ7.J631635Wh   1990   [E]   90-5559   ISBN 0-02-747845-9

I worry about my mother, 'cause I'm starting school tomorrow. As long as I've known my mom, I've never left her alone.

Do you think she'll miss me?
I hope she won't be scared without
me. But school starts tomorrow,
and I really have to go.

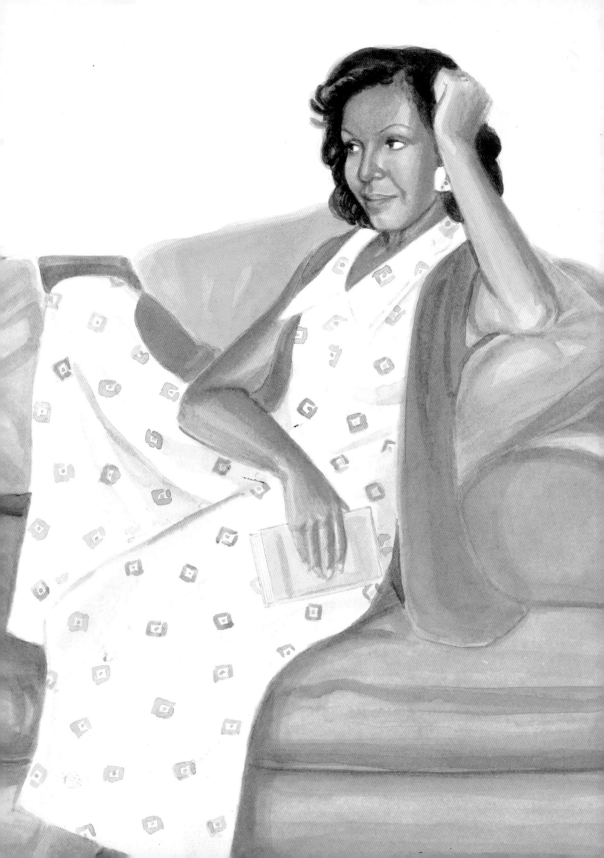

No more cooking muffins together. No more taking time with breakfast. I'll have to hurry and eat cold cereal. It never tastes as good.

We used to sing lots of songs together, like "The Fuzzy Wuzzy Bear" and "I'm a Little Teapot." Who'll remind her of the words when I'm gone?

Now Mom can't watch cartoons with me while we straighten up the living room. She'll have to spend the mornings all alone.

No more time for her to comb my hair in the morning. I won't have time to comb her hair for her, either.

No more helping her with the groceries.
You know she's never done it alone.

No more picture books. Mom loves to hear me read them. No more tea for two at three o'clock. But my bear, Miss Muffin, will still be there.

Oh, I've been to day-care centers. And I've stayed overnight with Grandma. But Mom and I have never been apart for very long.

My daddy tells me Mom will be all right by herself. But I tell him, "She won't be happy." He tells me Mom will make other friends. I say, "None as good as me."

I tell him, "Mom teaches me lots of
things. My ABC's, how to write my name." I
tell him, "She knows everything, except how
to get along without me."

I say, "Maybe you can stay home. If I can't stay here, why not you?" He said he would if he could, 'cause he misses Mommy, too.

Now I'll have to wake Mom in the morning.
Then I'll have to pick out my clothes every day.
My mom really loves to do that. Maybe I'll
still let her.

So Mom will walk me to school tomorrow. It will be like when we used to walk to the park together. But then I'll kiss her and hug her and tell her good-bye.

But I'll still worry about my mother. What will she do without me? Today she asked me to come closer so she could wipe my tears away.

My mom said, "I don't want you to leave me, baby, but school is such a great new adventure. You're going to be able to learn so much and do so much. There will be so many new things you can even teach me."

"Well, I'm not going to let you be lonely, Mom. When I come home, I'll tell you everything I've learned. I will bring you pictures I've drawn. I can bring over all my new friends. Maybe they can become your new friends, too."

"Well, you don't have to worry about me, sweetheart," said my mother. "Though I'll miss you, I won't be lonely. I'll be starting my own new adventure. While you're at school tomorrow, I'll be beginning a brand-new job."

"You know, Mom, maybe school won't be
so bad after all. Think of all the great new
things we can tell each other when we get home."
"I can hardly wait, baby."